Let's Go, Vikings!

Featuring
Viktor

Aimee Aryal
Illustrated by Miguel De Angel

www.mascotbooks.com

It was a beautiful fall day in the Twin Cities. Minnesota Vikings fans from all over The North Star State were making their way to the Metrodome for a football game. Everyone dressed in purple and gold.

As fans arrived at the Metrodome, they were greeted by the team's mascot, Viktor. Seeing Viktor, fans cheered, "Let's go, Vikings!"

Viktor made his way to the Metrodome Plaza, where Vikings fans were gathering before the game. The smell of good food was too much to resist as Viktor stopped for lunch. Happy to see the team's mascot, Vikings fans cheered, "Hello, Viktor!"

Viktor watched as some children, and even a few grown-ups, painted their faces for the game. As fans made their way into the Metrodome, they cheered, "Let's go, Vikings!"

On his way to the field, Viktor joined the team in the locker room. Players strapped on their pads and dressed in their Minnesota Vikings uniforms. Wearing purple and gold made each player feel proud to be a part of the Minnesota Vikings community.

The coach delivered final instructions and encouraged the team to play their best. The coach cheered, "Let's go, Vikings!"

It was now time for the Vikings to take the field. The announcer called, "Vikings fans, on your feet! Here are your Minnesota Vikings!" The team sprinted onto the field, with Viktor leading the way. It was very loud in the Metrodome!

Viktor and the players huddled around the team captains and cheered, "Let's go, Vikings!"

The team captains met at midfield for
the coin toss. The referee flipped a coin
high in the air and the visiting team called,
"Heads." The coin landed with the heads side
up – the Vikings would begin the game by
kicking off.

The referee reminded the players that
it was important to play hard, but also with
good sportsmanship.

The Vikings kicker booted the ball down the field to start the action. With the game underway, the kicker cheered, "Let's go, Vikings!"

After the opening kickoff, it was time for the
Vikings defense to take the field. Viktor led the crowd
in a "DE-FENSE" chant. Viktor held up the letter "D"
in one hand and a white picket fence in the other.
With the crowd's encouragement, the Vikings defense
sacked the quarterback. Fans roared with approval and
cheered, "Let's go, Vikings!"

After the defense did its job, the Vikings offense went to work. With great teamwork, they marched down the field and into scoring position. On fourth down, the team was only one yard away from the end zone.

"Let's go for it!" instructed the coach, and the quarterback called a play in the huddle.

The quarterback yelled, "Down. Set. Hike!" before handing the ball to the running back, who crossed the goal line.

TOUCHDOWN!

After the score, the crowd erupted with joy and fans cheered, "Let's go, Vikings!"

At the end of the first half, the Vikings headed back to the locker room. The coach stopped to answer a few questions from a television reporter. In the locker room, the team rested and prepared for the second half.

Meanwhile, Vikings fans, including Viktor, stretched their legs and picked up a few snacks at the concession stands. Everywhere Viktor went, fans cheered, "Let's go, Vikings!"

The action continued on the field in the second half. In the stands, fans were enjoying the game and the festive atmosphere. One little Vikings fan was eating a "Dome Dog" when everyone around her began pointing at the big screen. She looked up and saw herself on television. The little fan gave Viktor a high-five and cheered, "Let's go, Vikings!"

With only a few ticks of the clock remaining, the score was tied. The Vikings lined-up for a field goal try. After a good snap and a perfect hold, the kicker booted the ball toward the goal posts. The stadium was nearly silent as all eyes followed the flight of the ball.

The kick was good!

The Minnesota Vikings won the football game! The kicker cheered, "Let's go, Vikings!"

The Vikings and their fans celebrated the thrilling win. Viktor distracted the coach while players dumped water on him. Viktor sure was mischievous! The teams then shook hands and congratulated each other on a good game.

"See you next week, Viktor!" a family called as they left the Metrodome.

Everyone cheered, "Let's go, Vikings!"

For Anna and Maya ~ Aimee Aryal

For Sue, Ana Milagros, and Angel Miguel ~ Miguel De Angel

In light of the organization's commitment to community, the Viking Children's Fund (VCF) was established in 1978 and has raised $7.65 million to give back to those in need. The VCF is a means for Vikings players, coaches, cheerleaders, staff and their families to focus their community support to help children. The VCF distributes grants to health, education and family services organizations benefiting children. To learn more about the VCF, please visit vikings.com

A portion of the proceeds from the sale of this book will go to the Viking Children's Fund.

For more information, please contact Mascot Books,
P.O. Box 220157, Chantilly, VA 20153-0157

ISBN: 978-1-932888-99-7

Printed in the United States.

www.mascotbooks.com

www.mascotbooks.com

Title List

Team	Book Title	Author	Team	Book Title	Author
Baseball			**Pro Football**		
Boston Red Sox	Hello, Wally!	Jerry Remy	Carolina Panthers	Let's Go, Panthers!	Aimee Aryal
Boston Red Sox	Wally And His Journey Through Red Sox Nation!	Jerry Remy	Dallas Cowboys	How 'Bout Them Cowboys!	Aimee Aryal
			Green Bay Packers	Go, Packres, Go!	Aimee Aryal
New York Yankees	Let's Go, Yankees!	Yogi Berra	Kansas City Chiefs	Let's Go, Chiefs!	Aimee Aryal
New York Mets	Hello, Mr. Met!	Rusty Staub	Minnesota Vikings	Let's Go, Vikings!	Aimee Aryal
St. Louis Cardinals	Hello, Fredbird!	Ozzie Smith	New York Giants	Let's Go, Giants!	Aimee Aryal
Philadelphia Phillies	Hello, Phillie Phanatic!	Aimee Aryal	New England Patriots	Let's Go, Patriots!	Aimee Aryal
Chicago Cubs	Let's Go, Cubs!	Aimee Aryal	Seattle Seahawks	Let's Go, Seahawks!	Aimee Aryal
Chicago White Sox	Let's Go, White Sox!	Aimee Aryal	Washington Redskins	Hail To The Redskins!	Aimee Aryal
Cleveland Indians	Hello, Slider!	Bob Feller			
			Coloring Book		
			Dallas Cowboys	How 'Bout Them Cowboys!	Aimee Aryal
College					
Alabama	Hello, Big Al!	Aimee Aryal	Michigan State	Hello, Sparty!	Aimee Aryal
Alabama	Roll Tide!	Ken Stabler	Minnesota	Hello, Goldy!	Aimee Aryal
Arizona	Hello, Wilbur!	Lute Olsen	Mississippi	Hello, Colonel Rebel!	Aimee Aryal
Arkansas	Hello, Big Red!	Aimee Aryal	Mississippi State	Hello, Bully!	Aimee Aryal
Auburn	Hello, Aubie!	Aimee Aryal	Missouri	Hello, Truman!	Todd Donoho
Auburn	War Eagle!	Pat Dye	Nebraska	Hello, Herbie Husker!	Aimee Aryal
Boston College	Hello, Baldwin!	Aimee Aryal	North Carolina	Hello, Rameses!	Aimee Aryal
Brigham Young	Hello, Cosmo!	LaVell Edwards	North Carolina St.	Hello, Mr. Wuf!	Aimee Aryal
Clemson	Hello, Tiger!	Aimee Aryal	Notre Dame	Let's Go, Irish!	Aimee Aryal
Colorado	Hello, Ralphie!	Aimee Aryal	Ohio State	Hello, Brutus!	Aimee Aryal
Connecticut	Hello, Jonathan!	Aimee Aryal	Oklahoma	Let's Go, Sooners!	Aimee Aryal
Duke	Hello, Blue Devil!	Aimee Aryal	Oklahoma State	Hello, Pistol Pete!	Aimee Aryal
Florida	Hello, Albert!	Aimee Aryal	Penn State	Hello, Nittany Lion!	Aimee Aryal
Florida State	Let's Go, 'Noles!	Aimee Aryal	Penn State	We Are Penn State!	Joe Paterno
Georgia	Hello, Hairy Dawg!	Aimee Aryal	Purdue	Hello, Purdue Pete!	Aimee Aryal
Georgia	How 'Bout Them Dawgs!	Vince Dooley	Rutgers	Hello, Scarlet Knight!	Aimee Aryal
Georgia Tech	Hello, Buzz!	Aimee Aryal	South Carolina	Hello, Cocky!	Aimee Aryal
Illinois	Let's Go, Illini!	Aimee Aryal	So. California	Hello, Tommy Trojan!	Aimee Aryal
Indiana	Let's Go, Hoosiers!	Aimee Aryal	Syracuse	Hello, Otto!	Aimee Aryal
Iowa	Hello, Herky!	Aimee Aryal	Tennessee	Hello, Smokey!	Aimee Aryal
Iowa State	Hello, Cy!	Amy DeLashmutt	Texas	Hello, Hook 'Em!	Aimee Aryal
James Madison	Hello, Duke Dog!	Aimee Aryal	Texas A & M	Howdy, Reveille!	Aimee Aryal
Kansas	Hello, Big Jay!	Aimee Aryal	UCLA	Hello, Joe Bruin!	Aimee Aryal
Kansas State	Hello, Willie!	Dan Walter	Virginia	Hello, CavMan!	Aimee Aryal
Kentucky	Hello, Wildcat!	Aimee Aryal	Virginia Tech	Hello, Hokie Bird!	Aimee Aryal
Louisiana State	Hello, Mike!	Aimee Aryal	Virginia Tech	Yea, It's Hokie Game Day!	Frank Beamer
Maryland	Hello, Testudo!	Aimee Aryal	Wake Forest	Hello, Demon Deacon!	Aimee Aryal
Michigan	Let's Go, Blue!	Aimee Aryal	West Virginia	Hello, Mountaineer!	Aimee Aryal
			Wisconsin	Hello, Bucky!	Aimee Aryal
NBA					
Dallas Mavericks	Let's Go, Mavs!	Mark Cuban			
Kentucky Derby					
Kentucky Derby	White Diamond Runs For The Roses	Aimee Aryal			

More great titles coming soon!

info@mascotbooks.com

VIKINGS